RUMPELSTILTSKIN

To my mother

Copyright © 1997 by Marie-Louise Gay

Groundwood Books / Douglas & McIntyre Ltd.
585 Bloor Street West
Toronto, Ontario M6G 1K5

Distributed in the U.S.A. by Publishers Group West
4065 Hollis Street
Emeryville, CA 94608

The publisher gratefully acknowledges the assistance of the
Ontario Arts Council and the Canada Council.

Library of Congress data is available.

Canadian Cataloguing in Publication Data
Main entry under title:
Rumpelstiltskin
"A Groundwood book".
ISBN 0-88899-279-3
1. Fairy Tales. 2. Folklore - Germany. I. Grimm, Jacob, 1785-1863.
II. Grimm, Wilhelm, 1786-1859. III. Gay, Marie-Louise.
PZ8.R89G39 1997   j398.21'0943   C96-932189-9

The illustrations are done in graphite and colored pencils on vellum.
Printed and bound in China by Everbest Printing Co., Ltd.

THE BROTHERS GRIMM

RUMPELSTILTSKIN

MARIE-LOUISE GAY

A GROUNDWOOD BOOK ✴ DOUGLAS & McINTYRE ✴ TORONTO VANCOUVER BUFFALO

There was once
a miller who was poor, but
he had a beautiful daughter.

ONE DAY

he came to speak with the king and boasted
that his daughter could spin gold out of straw.

The king said to the miller, "If your
daughter is as clever as you say, bring her to
my castle tomorrow so that she can prove it."

WHEN

the girl was brought to the king, he led her into a
room full of straw and gave her a wheel and spindle.

"Now set to work," he said, "and if by the early
morning you have not spun this straw to gold, you
shall die." And he shut the door, and left her
there alone.

THE POOR MILLER'S

daughter was left there sitting. She had no idea
how to spin gold from straw, and her
distress grew so great that she began to weep.

All at once the door opened, and in came a
little man.

"Good evening, miller's daughter.
Why are you crying?"

"Oh!" answered the girl. "I have to spin gold
out of straw, and I don't know how."

"What will you give me if I spin it for you?"
 the little man asked.

"My necklace," said the girl.

THE LITTLE MAN

took the necklace, seated himself before the wheel, and *whirr, whirr, whirr!* Three times round and the bobbin was full. Then he took up another, and *whirr, whirr, whirr!* Three times round and that was full.

And so he went on till the morning, when all the straw had been spun, and all the bobbins were full of gold.

At sunrise the king came in, and when he saw the gold, he was astonished and very happy, for he was an extremely greedy man.

HE TOOK

the miller's daughter into another room filled
with straw. It was much bigger than the first
one, and he told her that if she valued her life,
she must spin all the straw into gold in
one night.

The girl did not know what to do, so she
began to cry. The door opened, and the little
man appeared.

"What will you give me if I spin all this straw
into gold?" he asked.

"The ring from my finger," answered the girl.

So the little man

took the ring and began again to send the wheel whirring round.

By the next morning all the straw had been spun into glistening gold.

The king was happy beyond measure at the sight, but he could never have enough gold, so he took the miller's daughter into an even larger room full of straw.

"This, too, must be spun in one night," he said, "and if you accomplish this, you shall be my wife."

Although she was only a miller's daughter, he thought he was not likely to find anyone richer in the whole world.

As soon as the girl

was alone, the little man appeared for the third time. "What will you give me if I spin the straw for you this time?" he asked.

"I have nothing left to give," answered the girl.

"Then you must promise me the first child you have after you are queen," said the little man.

Who knows whether that will happen? thought the girl, and she promised the little man. He began to spin, until all the straw was gold.

In the morning the king came. When he found everything done according to his wish, he ordered that the wedding be held at once, and the miller's daughter became a queen.

In a year's time

she brought a fine child into the world, and she thought no more of the little man. Then one day he suddenly appeared in the garden.

"Now give me what you promised me," he said.

The queen was terrified. She offered the little man all the riches of the kingdom if he would only leave the child.

"No," he said. "I would rather have something living than all the treasures of the world."

Then the queen began to weep, and the little man had pity on her.

"I will give you three days," he said. "If at the end of that time you cannot tell me my name, you must give up the child to me."

THE QUEEN

spent the whole night thinking over all the names that she had ever heard. She sent a messenger through the land to ask far and wide for all the names that could be found.

When the little man came the next day, she repeated all the names she knew, beginning with Caspar, Melchior and Balthazar. She went through the whole list, but after each one the little man said, "That is not my name."

THE SECOND DAY

the queen sent the messenger to find out what all
the servants were called, and she told the man the
most unusual names.

"Perhaps you are called Roastribs," she asked. "Or
Sheepshanks, or Spindleshanks?"

But he answered nothing except, "That is not
my name."

THE THIRD DAY

the messenger came back again. "I have not been able to find one single new name," he said. "But as I passed through the woods, I came to a high hill, and near it was a little house. Before the house burned a fire, and round the fire danced a comical little man who hopped on one leg and cried,

"'Today I bake, tomorrow I brew,
The day after that the queen's child comes in.
And, oh! I am glad that nobody knew
That the name I am called is Rumpelstiltskin!'"

YOU CAN IMAGINE

how pleased the queen was to hear this. Soon afterward,
the little man walked in.

"Now, Mrs. Queen," he said. "What is my name?"

"Are you called Jack?" she asked.

"No," he answered.

"Are you called Harry?" she asked.

"No," he answered.

Then she said, "So perhaps your name is..."

RUMPELSTI

"THE DEVIL
told you that! The devil told you that!" cried
the little man, and in his anger he stamped his
right foot so hard that it went right into the
ground above his knee. Then he seized his left
foot with both his hands in such a fury that he
split in two, and that was the end of him.